# A Life For A Purse

## Chapter 1

Noel felt her heart beat faster. The green cubicles around her seemed taller than usual. Her coworkers were carrying on their conversations with their own customers through the walls. With nothing but green walls surrounding her, she felt like she was in a prison. She took her fingers off of the keyboard. One of her hands touched a piece of paper right next to her paper coffee cup.

"That's not going to do shit, you dumb bitch." The man's voice was mad and shaky. If Noel could guess, then the man was probably old enough to be her grandfather. In the upper right hand corner of her computer screen, Noel read eight minutes on the timer and not the twenty minutes like she thought.

The old man continued throwing a variety of insults at her. The drawings on the paper were a collection of yarn and teddy bears dressed in various clothing. Noel wrote a shopping list on the side of the paper with Wal-Mart at the end of the list. She stared at that paper, looking forward to her shift ending and for her heart to start beating at a normal speed.

"I'm sorry sir. Please say that again." Immediately, Noel wished she could take back her words.

"Dumb and deaf too? I've been a customer for years. Are you kidding me? The customer service here has

# A Life For A Purse

"S-sir...I can't cancel your service." Why couldn't this man just listen? Canceling someone's service required her to forward this call to someone above her position.

"Excuse you? I want a real solution. I'm not getting on my old ass knees. That routers on the floor, bitch. Do you understand me? You clearly don't."

The timer showed twelve minutes now. Her supervisor was still away from his desk. Was every word out of the customer's mouth really important? Noel firmly pressed on the end call button. The old man's insults abruptly ended mid-sentence. Her heart slowed down to a normal pace.

What could she do now while she waited for another call? Noel laid back against her hard chair, looking at the piece of paper right next to her coffee cup. "Why am I here?" A small ring brought her out of her thoughts. The supervisor's status read available. A window appeared on screen with his name at the top of the window.

"Good evening Noel White."

Noel placed her hands on the keyboard and quickly typed a response. "Yes?"

"Turn your status on break and come into the main office"

# A Life For A Purse

Noel lazily waved her hand to a coworker who was walking around with two cups of coffee. Mike smiled but quickly frowned and kept walking. Was it that obvious she was in trouble? The reflection in the front of the main office's wooden doors' window caused her to stop. Her skin was whiter; her long hair had random dirt in its strands, and there were bags underneath her brown eyes.

What happened to her hygiene?

"Noel White." In the room, she could see her team leader sitting by one of the chairs next to the wooden, oval table. "I want you to take a seat."

"Sure thing." She stepped into the office and pulled the chair in front of him and sat.

"What's going on? You disconnected a call." Pence took a pencil from the folds of his ear and began tapping it on a stack of papers. Noel White was written on top of those papers.

Noel's eyes grew wide; she did do that a few minutes ago.

"You do realize that we do monitor each and every single call? I know that you do realize this!" Tapping the pencil faster, Pence shook his head.

Why lie? Recording customers' calls was one of the first things she and others went through while going through training.

# A Life For A Purse

"You should also remember how we grade each call. Sounds like I'm regurgitating the same garbage you've already learned and should already remember. " Pence quit tapping the pen and put the pen into his chest pocket.

"I know that. He wasn't listening."

Her supervisor clasped his hands together and placed his hands over his gut. "What do you think you've could have done instead of ruining a long time customer relationship? "

The paper also had a long list of grades; grades that were below expectations. Noel grimaced. "I could have continued to tell him to unplug the router and… then replug it back in?"

"That's not wrong." Pence leaned back in his chair. Was he contemplating her answer that deeply? "Or you could have escalated the call."

"You were away from your desk."

"That was one solution. What was Mike doing? What about Whitney? Harold? Jonathon?"

Knowing what the sky looked, while she sat at her cubicle, was already a problem.

"I don't know." Noel held both of her hands on the leather arm rest of her chair.

"Could you have told the customer to wait while you research a better solution?" Pence tapped the top of this pen.

# A Life For A Purse

What was a better solution? Noel was finding it hard to keep her composure while under this test. At least she was no longer spacing out. Pence's wrinkled face was vividly in front of her. Of all the things to focus on. "If I could research how to get him to listen. I would have."

Pence opened his mouth but then he paused. "You look like you need a break. It's slow here. You should go home now."

Noel glanced at the clock hanging on the wall in front of her, "B-but it's only three and my shift ends at five."

"I know. I know Noel. Believe me, we all know." He was back to tapping the pen on his stacks of papers.

Noel stared at the low grades again, "Why are you constantly sending me home?"

Pence's eyes widened, "Again. It's slow. It's really slow and you look really, really worn out. I'm afraid you might pass out."

Phones rang left and right outside of the office's walls. "Are you sure?"

Pence took the papers and smiled. "Come back tomorrow and start the day fresh."

There was six months left on her contract. "Ok." Noel stood up from her chair feeling that the conversation was over.

# A Life For A Purse

"Good. Everyone will see you tomorrow."

---

While holding her phone and staring into the screen, Noel sat in her car. Leaving home early while the phones were constantly ringing loud and clear? She was leaving early for the third time this month. Had anyone else besides her ever left before their shift ended?

Where would Noel drive her car to this time? Would she go to the Wendy's or buy something from the store? If anyone at her home saw her before five, there would be Hell. At least she could waste time in Wal-Mart. When it was five o' clock she could leave.

A drop of water fell on to her front window. It's raining. If her location in the office was not secluded maybe she would have noticed and took her umbrella from underneath her desk. Noel made her choice to drive to Wal-Mart. There were always cheaper options for food in that store.

A vibration on the left side of her hip interrupted her thoughts as she began driving out of her parking space. Noel drove her car back into the parking space and turned it off. She tapped answer on her phone screen.

"This is Angie Hawthorn from Reynard Systems. Is this Noel I'm speaking with?" What could her temp agency be calling about now? They already gave her enough tips to perform better at this job.

"Yes, this is Noel White. Hello Hawthorn."

# A Life For A Purse

"Good. We wanted to let you know things weren't working for you at White Wolf. Mr. Pence is thankful for your time with his company. He says you've been a great help and…"

"But that's not right! My contract's for another six months. He told me there was a lot to do." She gripped the stirring wheel hard.

There was a long silence on the phone. "Noel. Your performance was not even at or above acceptable. Pence gave you a lot of chances and today was the last straw. On top of that, we've placed you in other positions. Pence is the only manager who's said anything remotely positive about you."

The papers on the table were beginning to make sense. Was there a way to save herself? "What did I do wrong? I came in early and I wore the best professional outfits I could buy."

Hawthorne made a disgusted sound. "I told you there's no need to dress up for White Wolf. If you're uncomfortable behind the phones then the customers will feel that."

Noel looked herself down, wishing she could put on some black jeans before she left the house. "D-don't you have anything else for me?"

Another long pause again. "You have your Security+ certification. You're a…smart and talented girl. I'll call you again, ok?"

# A Life For A Purse

Granted the beauty of being behind the phone, Noel slumped into her chair. "O-ok."

"All right?"

The call ended before Noel fully realized that Hawthorn wanted a response.

Was the Internet Technology field really for her? Three jobs from Reynard Systems and no permanent placement like Angie promised?

Rain hit her car hard. Noel shook in her seat at the sudden down pour. Was she still going to Wal-Mart? Water covered her window, making it hard to see even the cars parked in front of her.

Noel rubbed her forehead and then ran her hair through her bangs, down to the back of her head. "No..." Her umbrella was still inside of her old cubical.

She still had her security badge with her. Like all the other jobs, Noel knew she would have to turn this back in at some point. Why not now instead of later. Her umbrella?

If today was yesterday then Noel would have been concerned. She was wearing a black suit and not the white dress she wore yesterday. Noel opened the car and ran across the street. At four, there was a chance that some coworkers were on break or walking around the building looking for a good place to smoke.

# A Life For A Purse

The glass sliding doors flew open after Noel scanned her badge against the security door. The security guard eyed her and then went back to resting his head on the palm of his hand.

She had tripped on the smoothed floor leading toward the double wooden doors. It was pitch black through the windows of the closed, wooden doors. Pence couldn't be in there.

Finally, Noel walked through the hallway leading to the room with her old cubical. Small droplets of water hit the carpet. She didn't realize the rain had soaked her clothing this badly.

"What's up Noel. All the online stores are doing Cyber Week. Can you believe it? Did you catch any good deals too?" Mike walked forward with his cup of coffee in one hand. "It's raining outside? Hey!"

Noel walked past him. Mike was always the talkative type. Cyber Week? This was the last thing she wanted to be reminded of now that she was running low on money.

Everything was as it was in her cubical. She took the coaster, then the drawing she was working on, and then the umbrella. Water dripped on to her desk but she did not feel like cleaning it up at all.

Putting the paper inside of her soaked pockets would ruin the paper and the drawings she had on them. Her movement was fast and out of the area before any other

# A Life For A Purse

former coworker could see her or suspect that she was being let go.

Noel felt her adrenaline going. At her last job, two men approached her and escorted her out of the building in front of everyone. That incident was not going to happen this time.

Stopping by the entrance, she looked at the security guard. Holding her items close to her, she took her badge off of her shirt and handed it to the security guard.

The guard looked up, raising his eyebrows. "What is this Sweaty?" Noel looked around. There was no one in sight. The security guard looked in the same directions. "Excuse me?"

"It's my badge." Why couldn't he just take the badge? She held the badge closer.

"I know it's your badge but why are you handing me this? I thought you kids would be here for a long while."

That burned for a bit.

"Um..." Footsteps were coming from the hallway.

"Isn't that a lot of money, Mike?" Was that Whitney?

"Who cares? That laptop is half off and I'm going to splurge like nobody's business."

Mike and Whitney were getting closer.

# A Life For A Purse

"Somethings don't work out." Not wanting to cause a scene, Noel dropped the security badge on his desk and headed for the door.

"You're a sweat girl, Noel. God bless you."

Noel had no idea where she was driving to. There were cars driving bumper to bumper, trapping her traffic. Noel realized that she was in the wrong lane. Was she going home or was she still headed for Wal-Mart?

There were a few opportunities to switch to another lane but another car would fill up that gap immediately. Why was she in this middle lane? The fastest way to her cousin's house was through the right lane. The very lane she was in lead to her mother's house. Noel gripped the stirring wheel again. The last thing she wanted was to be anywhere near that woman.

A gap opened to the right of her. She immediately filled that spot and entered the right lane, ignoring an angry horn or two.

After making her turn, traffic lessened. Her home was not far away. A crumbled piece of paper from her cup holder hit her knee. She smiled at it. Surprisingly, the paper had remained dry while being in her closed hand as she walked out of White Wolf.

# A Life For A Purse

Cars were driving close together again a few lights before she could reach her cousin's house. This was perfect timing. The light turned red. Noel turned off her windshield wipers. Seeing no rain drops, she opened her window on her side and firmly pressed on her breaks.

Another car took the open spot Noel created. All of the man's windows were down. Rap music, in conjunction with the man's base, caused a vibration on the road. He moved his head to the music until the music grew feint.

"You didn't think we were done with Black Friday and Cyber Monday? This week is our biggest sales of yet! From exotic name brands to purses that will make everyone jealous. All for fifteen to fifty percent off! Come visit us at Jessicas.com for more information."

Why did everyone need to turn their radio up so loud? What was the point?

"Look where you're going? Fuck you homeless assholes!" The same driver threw a soda cup at an old man with a sign in his hands. The hobo did not flinch. Instead, he held the cardboard sign tighter with shaky hands.

Five for a sandwich? The sign was on the verge of falling apart. The man made his way across the street and stood on the sidewalk, pointing his sign toward every car. Each driver and their passengers pretending to look elsewhere. Noel frowned.

The light turned green and she turned into her neighborhood.

# A Life For A Purse

Noel was not allowed to park at her cousin's house. Her cousin's driveway did hold room for four cars. Stephanie told her parking on the curb would be easier for both her and her husband. Noel drove further down and to the other side of the street where she could park close to a nearby curb.

Parking the car next to the curb, Noel stared at her car door, appreciating the traffic. The traffic spared her from going into her cousin's house sooner than her old shift was supposed to end.

Just Roy's truck was on the driveway. Her cousin's husband worked at night so she did not need to tell him the news yet. She turned the keys in the door and walked inside.

The paper had been clutched tightly in the palms of her hands. Her family would have to find out sometime. She walked up the stairs. Noel was not in a rush to tell her family members like she used to. Already, she could hear her disappointed mother's voice like with the last time she was let go.

Her bed was white, her room was white, and her carpet was white. The only things of color was Noel's table in the colorful fabrics and various other materials on her table. Even the wooden table was painted white. Noel placed the paper on the hard wood and pulled her white chair close to the table.

Spreading the paper open, Noel opened her laptop. The laptop screen lit up, leaving off on a screen full of

# A Life For A Purse

homemade items. Photos of pillows, painted jars, and stuffed animals lined up across the webpage. Stuff she handcrafted in her limited spare time.

Something caught her attention at the top of Creative Heaven's webpage. An icon depicting one new message marked by a red one in a white circle at the right side of the homepage. Noel clicked on the message, smiling at the long list of excited customers wanting their orders soon. Unlike tech support, she felt she could handle these questions without blanking out.

"NoelandCreations,

Hello. My name's JasmineSmith. I am so, so mad I missed out on those one-of-a-kind scented stuffed bears. I had really especially loved the blue one with the life jacket. That was so adorable.

This might be too much. I see that your store never carries the same item twice. It's been two months and I haven't seen the cuties again. I know you don't take commissions but I'll pay no matter what the price is. Please?"

Was this a joke? Noel began typing on the keyboard.

"Sorry but I still don't take commissions. I have another job that takes a lot of time." Noel hit the backspace button, "Hello, I'm glad you loved the scented bears. I loved making them. "

# A Life For A Purse

Noel minimized the window and began hovering her mouse over various folders on her desktop screen. Where was the file? Would other people want commissions from her too?

Finally, Noel found the folder titled Commissions. This was the folder? When was the last time she looked inside of this folder?

The insides of the folder held several files for teddy bears, pillows, and blankets. She double clicked on the teddy bear file. Thirteen commissions done so far typed at the top of the screen.

What perfect timing if this was a real request. Below that information was typical stuff such as name, address information, and phone number. The commission price was three hundred dollars. These teddy bears were huge, wore clothing, and took a lot of her time.

Noel copied the contents inside of the commission file and placed that information into the message. She hit the send button.

Other messages read thank you for the order.

Time at White Wolf had caused her to stop checking notification on Creative Heaven. There was barely any time to handcraft a small teddy bear or pillow. In order to focus on landing a permanent position with White Wolf, Noel had stopped making homemade items. Before stopping, she had accidentally sowed a few needles into her stuffed animals and then sold them on this website. That was a safety hazard.

# A Life For A Purse

Noel hopped that those items was only going to adults who would not squeeze the stuffed animals. Maybe it was good she didn't have to deal with angry customers over the phone.

When she was younger, crafting homemade items was just a hobby to kill boredom while her single mother was at work.

Another message popped up on the dashboard. Noel saw that the message was from the same user. That commission form was filled perfectly. Another message appeared, informing her that three hundred dollars was sent to her account. Was this really happening?

Noel opened her paper and looked at the long list of items she needed for her business. How much would she have to pay before she could replace all the material she once had at her mother's house?

A car light went through her window blinds. Noel frowned. Stephanie stepped out of the parked car, in a business suit, and continued to walk toward her door. Not wanting to deal with any questions, Noel walked over to her bed, laid on top of it and fell asleep.

Will she get another job soon?

## Chapter 2

# A Life For A Purse

*Noel wiped the tears from her eyes. She held her teddy bear's head in her hands. Juice stained its purple fur and paper fell off of it in chunks. Was this the same teddy bear she spent a whole week to make?*

*"This wasn't trash!" All of her clothes and other belongings were inside of her cousin's new car. Everything except her sewing materials and everything she listed on Creative Heaven. That was with the trash man.*

*Her mother stood in front of her, helping her cousin stand up. Stephanie cried out in pain, holding her eye. "My face! She hit me. I can't come into work like this."*

*"Who cares?" Noel stood up, dropping her teddy bear's head. Her cousin stepped back and screamed. If there was something she wanted to do more, she was going to punch her cousin again and again.*

*Her mother pulled her cousin behind her. "Not on my property. You two are getting in the car like the daughters I raised you to be. Noel?"*

*How could she get pass her mother? Stephanie took a few steps back and then she ran to the driver's seat of her car.*

*"That was my work. It's not trash!" Some of those lost items needed to be shipped off to customers after moving in with Stephanie. What was she going to do now?*

*A slap brought her back into reality. "You would have never been fired if you stopped working on your fake business. Get in the car and stop playing with toys."*

# A Life For A Purse

Noel searched Reynard Systems' website. Why would she bother with this temp agency again? Reynard Systems was a building full of broken promises. Other job websites did exist for her to upload her resume to. She moved her phone in hands, disliking the results from her search. Her fingers hovered over her contacts. One of the contacts was her friend Cindy Hamilton.

Maybe there were other temporary job websites she could apply to.

"Hello. Noel? Are you there?"

"What? Cindy? Is that you?" Noel held her smartphone to her face. She indeed accidentally called her best friend. "This is White Wolf...I'm sorry Cindy." She was not working anymore. When was she going to realize this?

"White Wolf? Isn't that you're job? You're calling me at your job?" Cindy laughed.

Noel stared at her laptop's screen. "Um...I don't work at White Wolf anymore."

The laughing stopped. "You don't? What the hell happened? You were there for a long time!"

"I know. Something's happen, I guess." Noel held the phone to her ear.

"Something's happen? Noel White? Don't you want to escape your arrogant cousin? I'd go crazy if I was

# A Life For A Purse

stuck in that creepy white room for any longer than a week."

"It's been two years with my cousin."

"Feels like five, Noel. You're family treats you like crap. But you need a full time job if you want to stay with me. I don't think IT is your thing."

"It's not." Noel's voice was weak.

"It's not? It's really not? Really?"

Noel almost pressed the end call button but this was her best friend. "I hate it and I got this stupid certification for nothing."

"You spent all that time studying for that shit? We could have been at the clubs. I know you haven't been to one…ever."

"What's the point? I don't care, Cindy." The to-do list fell by her feet. Noel quickly picked it up.

"I worked hard in order to get my mom to leave me alone. That didn't last long." Heat immediately rushed to Noel's cheeks.

"That's terrible. What she did was horrible."

"It didn't help that my cousin was helping the whole time. I lost a lot of my stuff that day. She didn't care how many hours I put into those pillows, the bears, or who wanted to buy them. I had to cancel so many orders." The

# A Life For A Purse

dirty teddy bear head had to go in to the trash as well that day.

"If I was there. I wouldn't had cared if she was your mother. Or if I was twenty two. She would have lost some teeth. I still love the small pillows you made for me. They're always on my bed."

Noel hovered over the feedback rating on her account. "I'm surprised I'm still allowed on this website. I couldn't even focus on anything for a long while. It took me some time to get back into sewing."

There was a long pause between the both of them. Dead air. A term that Noel would no longer have to remember. "You think you can make more money off of your hobby? Don't let what your cousin says get to you. I think if you lived with me, you could make your hobby into a real thing."

Noel closed her browser. "I don't know. I need to focus."

"Noel! Focus on your business. I'm not your mother. I'm not hackling you to get some crappy certification you don't want. I just need you to be happy. Happy."

"Right…I'm sorry. I guess I'll listen to music like I used to."

"Yes, you do that. I need to get back to the kids. I'll text you throughout the day. Just hang in there, Noel?"

# A Life For A Purse

"I'll try," Noel remembered something, "a woman wanted a commission from me today."

"A-A commission? I thought you don't do those anymore!" Cindy yelled, excited. "I'm really glad. You should really keep up with that app. I'll text you throughout the day tomorrow. I gotta go."

"Goodnight, Cindy."

No one was in the kitchen but herself. Noel reached into the refrigerator and pulled out the milk for her cereal. Placing the milk on the table next to her bowl, she sat down.

Noel put a spoonful of cereal into her mouth. The cereal was not a name brand but a knock off brand. This was not the cereal she told her cousin that she wanted. She wished she could go down to the store and buy some cereal with sugar in it. There was barely any sugar in the chocolate cereal.

She opened the bank app on her phone and quickly logged in. Three thousand dollars in her savings account? A smile almost appeared on her face but that smile disappeared. Noel recalled one old email which told her about her upcoming school loan payment. That was nearly three hundred dollars.

# A Life For A Purse

Her finger hovered over the information in her Creation Heaven app. The client readily paid three hundred dollars for her work. Maybe she could travel to Wal-Mart and finally buy every sewing supply that was thrown away? That would take a lot of money. Noel needed to buy what materials she needed to get this commission done.

Her other bank account suffered. Not the ten thousand she was hoping for. What happened? She clicked on a drop down arrow and looked at her recent purchases. Lots of times spent eating at restaurants, fast food and music for her phone. Only five hundred in that account?

Noel spent a lot of money on this smartphone so she could get use Creative Heaven and listen to unlimited music. Music was something that she would have to hold back on if she wanted to save money. She sighed and put another spoonful of cereal in her mouth.

Why did her cousin buy this off brand cereal? Why was she not allowed to paint her room or put posters on the wall? Noel asked herself that every day.

Roy was coming down the stairs slowly and dragging his feet heavily on the steps. Noel continued eating expecting Roy to get something to drink and leave.

"Noel? This is awkward." He sounded shocked.

Noel turned around but Roy was gone. The closet door by the entrance was open. Noel shrugged and put another spoonful into her mouth.

# A Life For A Purse

"No seriously!  What are you doing here?"  There was a level of concern which made Noel put down her spoon.

Roy walked back into the kitchen in a green robe. He took another step forward, pulling up a chair and then sitting down.

"It's an off day at my job?"

"That's not right at all.  I used to work there.  That place honors holidays.  No exceptions."  Roy shook his head.

That was correct.  "That was a long time ago. Companies change all the time, don't they?"

"We're paying for you living here.  I'd expect the truth from a 26-year-old woman."  Roy hit the table.

"Twenty six? I'm twenty five.  I'm a Christmas baby, remember?"  Noel's cheeks burned.

Roy sat there, staring at her intensely.  "I can't forget.  Steph reminds everyday every December till Christmas.  You're still a full grown woman underneath mine and Steph's roof."

"Reynard Systems let me go, yesterday."  Lying was not working out for her.

That intense gaze softened, "Why?"

"I don't know."

# A Life For A Purse

"I'm not surprised. You were always coming home early. That never bothered you?" There was that concern again. Noel stopped herself from shuddering.

"I always thought it was weird."

"Six months? How long do you have before that Security+ of yours expires?"

Noel lightly pushed the bowl from herself. Her appetite was gone. "A few months."

Roy stood up. He walked over to the sank, holding a huge cup underneath the faucet. Water ran through the filter and into his cup. "I'd use that time. You obtained that through a course right? Like I did."

Noel held the bowl and stood up from her spot. "I used a practice exam with a lot of questions from the real exam."

Roy shook his head. "That's seriously…illegal. You know that, right? What you did is called brain dumping. People are getting caught for that these days."

"These days?" A friend in college gave her a flash drive with the questions. She took the flash drive, wanting a quicker way than paying attention in her Security class.

Roy made his way toward the kitchen's entrance. "I have a huge collection of legal material in my office. I'd suggest using it because I want kids. Those kids need to sleep somewhere and my office or my bedroom is not the place." He walked up the stairs.

# A Life For A Purse

Noel just watched, not sure what to think of the conversation she just had. After all, she had no passion for the Information Technology field. It was a field which offered jobs in abundance in Virginia. Having a Security+ gave her more opportunities in Information Technology.

Stephanie was arriving home at seven. Noel pushed her chair but slowly into the table. Her cheeks were still heated.

She was already dressed. Knowing that White Wolf was a casual place, jeans, her white shirt, and a jacket passed for proper attire.

Noel decided to make her way to Wal-Mart this time. She was greeted by Christmas singing as he made her way toward Wal-Mart. A woman stood by the door, ringing her bell up and down. Noel reached for her wallet in her back pocket but then she stopped, smiled and then kept going. The scorn from the woman said enough.

Every penny counted. The last check from Reynard Systems was coming in for next week.

Kids ran past her followed by angry parents. Some customers walked shoulder to shoulder in some aisles. Maneuvering around these people, Noel stepped into the crowd and carefully began pushing her cart.

# A Life For A Purse

Noel saw a break in the line near the sewing section. Who else would buy sewing materials for Christmas? The section was completely empty except for a Walmart employee behind a counter who was looking at a sheet full of barcodes.

There was a large assortment of yarn lined up in one pile. Sorting through, Noel picked through the threads and found a nice green ball of cotton. The client did not say what color she preferred. Most of her teddy bears were traditional bear colors; dark brown, white, black, and grey.

But only a few bears were made with blue and green yarn. A few customers did buy those bears immediately. Why not a green bear this time? The customer filled out the form which said any color, even pink if she wanted.

This was a very excited fan she was dealing with. Noel lightly placed the yarn into her cart. What was next was the scents and this customer wanted lavender. At least the customer did decide to give her some guidance there.

Noel headed into the traffic again. The traffic lessened near the grocery section. The only way there would be deals on food if the food was close to expiring. The scents were on a collection right next to the new organic food section.

Wal-Mart had everything. Mom and pop shops used to have all the scents that she needed before Wal-Mart killed them. Noel picked up the lavender leaves, glad what the cash registers were not far away.

# A Life For A Purse

Much to her dismay, there was a long line at the self-checkout lane, eliminating the reason that she always entered this lane. Nine people in one line before she could pick a register of her own?

In front of her were children already holding their Christmas toys and parents trying their best to lie to them. Telling them that the toys were not their Christmas presents. Also in front of her were people with carts full of random small objects. There were only eight registers that were occupied with similar people. Was she the only one with a small handful of items?

A vibration on her side caused her to jump. Noel quickly took her phone out of her side holder. The screen had her mother's name at the top. Noel stared at her phone until the vibration stopped. Watching this line was not a bad idea after all.

One customer entered and picked a self-check out register. Noel took a couple of steps forward and stopped. Her phone started vibrating again. She repeated her same process again and then the phone stopped vibrating. Her phone vibrated but only for a second. What was this?

A message appeared on the screen, telling her to call her as soon as possible. One of the terrible things Noel did was get her mother to embrace texting.

Noel unlocked her phone and began texting a reply back but her mother called midway and her finger slid over the accept button.

# A Life For A Purse

"How did you ruin a perfectly good opportunity again? What did you do this time? Stephanie is mad, I'm furious. Are you disappointed because I am?" Despite the low volume on her phone, her mother's voice was loud.

Noel looked around. Two customers had already walked into the lane. Unconsciously, she had moved a few steps and stopped. "The contract ended early."

A scoff. "Oh...you said that with the last jobs. You're wasting your certification. What did you wear there?"

Noel moved a few spaces, enjoying the sudden pace of the line. "What does that matter?"

"What did you wear?"

Noel shook her head, "I worked behind the phone; not a cash register."

"I don't give a fuck, Noel. You're a White. Sometimes I'm surprised I gave birth to you. Did you wear your poor excuse for clothing? I've told you time and time again that no company in their right mind would like a woman working in anything less than professional clothing. That's not right."

Noel was finally at the front of the line. People in front of her were looking around, others were hiding smirks, and the cashier was frowning. Were they listening?

"Mike and even Whitney wore whatever they felt like wearing." Why did she blurt that out?

# A Life For A Purse

"I hate repeating myself.  How many times do I have to tell you that you're supposed to dress professionally no matter what that manager says the dress code is?  That is why they let you go.  If you had any questions about proper dress attire then you should have asked Stephanie -"

"Ma'am!  Ma'am!"

A few shouts brought Noel out of her conversation and back to watching the cashier wave at her.  Noel smiled and pushed her cart toward the cash register.  She finally started scanning her materials one by one.

"Do you understand me?"

"What?  I'm in Wal-Mart."

Her mother let out a long angry sigh.  "Oh my God.  Buying what?"

"Stephanie needed some groceries."  Noel took a ball of yarn from her cart and scanned the barcode.

"Oh…that's something you're doing right.  I thought you wasting your money on junk, again."

"I always buy what I need now, mom."

"Go talk to your cousin.  I hope she expresses her disappointment as well.  Goodbye."

Noel stopped scanning the last of her items and looked at her reflection through the scanner's glass surface.  There were still bags underneath her eyes.  She barely stayed up past eleven but the tiredness was there.

# A Life For A Purse

Noel paid for her materials and then she left.

"Life gets better sweaty. Don't let anything or anyone pull you down." The store associate smiled at her. Noel forced a smile on her face and left.

Stephanie wanted an explanation as well? Noel made her way to room, passing the bathroom. The shower was on, was that Roy or Stephanie? All the contents were on her table. Noel sat at her table and stared at her purchases. The conversation had sapped her of her energy. The rushing water stopped.

There was a knock at the side of the door. "Hey! What the hell? You were fired again? Underneath my roof?"

Stephanie stood by the doorway, grinding her teeth.

"They... ended my contract." Noel regretted leaving her room open. Was this the fourth time already? Could she get to sewing her stuffed animal now?

"Mother already told me. To help her out, I told her all the shitty outfits you wore."

Noel stood up from her bed, "That's not true. I wore dresses too." Dresses she often shifted positions in while talking on the phone.

# A Life For A Purse

Stephanie folded her arms. "Once every blue moon. I saw you in jeans more than ever. At my job, I'd be written up if I came in that garbage."

"You're a receptionist. My supervisor told me to stop over dressing so I could make better calls."

"God, I forget you're a woman sometimes."

Noel rolled her eyes. Was she really spending time having this conversation?

"My husband is a bad influence on you. Always walking around in clothes with holes in them. I've been meaning to throw those away for him."

"I get it. I get it. I've been looking for jobs, already." Noel moved her hand to open her laptop but her hand touched her Wal-Mart bag. The bag opened, allowing a ball of yarn to roll over to her laptop.

"Are you rebuilding that collection again?"

"What collection?"

"That garbage on my table."

"It's not garbage. That's for a client."

Stephanie threw her arms up in the air. "That pretend business? You're still keeping…? I was so proud of you when I saw you weren't making anything."

# A Life For A Purse

Noel forward her eyebrows and stood up from her chair. Stephanie stopped leaning against the wall. Her cousin stepped back. Worry was written all over her face.

"Pretend business?"

"I-I'm going to bed. I'll continue this conversation tomorrow." Stephanie turned around and left.

Noel took a deep breath and pulled out her phone from her back pocket. There was no good that would come from beating up her cousin. Her phone vibrated. She walked over to her bed, laid on it, and opened her text message app. There were several messages.

"Hi Noel! I wish I had a day off. These children never run out of energy here."

The next one. "I'm trying to concentrate since I'm on break."

"How's the commission work going? I know you can do it. I'm rooting for you."

"I'm so tired. The children started fighting over their Christmas treats again and I had to be the one to stop them and take care of the mess."

"Are you there? I know you can at least text back. Ah well. I don't want to come over there. I really don't but I will if it will cheer you up."

That was the last text. Noel thought of a reply but instead hovered her finger over the Creative Heaven app and took a look. There was no more messages.

# A Life For A Purse

The app had not finished loading. Her finger slipped and she pressed on an ad by mistake. That was one of the bad things about the app. Ads were constantly popping up at random moments.

The page loaded, giving her an article about four people murdered during Black Friday shopping. Images of shattered glass and crying women were placed throughout the article. A video of a woman screaming about the incident auto played. Noel closed the web browser not bothering to read about the whole article. Black Friday was a mistake as far as Noel was concerned.

Reading part of the article left Noel feeling uneasy. She started looking over her text messages again. "Just give me some time. I'll think of something. Shoot, can you make me something too? You know I don't care what it is. I'll pay you."

"You don't have to pay me...." Noel erased that sentence. She thought of a response but her eyelids grew heavy and she fell asleep.

The next few days was devoted to the commissions and job searching. She remembered her sketchbooks and her headphones underneath her bed. Noel took one of the pencils from her sketchbook and began drawing mockup sketches. Two commission requests in such a short time?

# A Life For A Purse

Stephanie had gone to work and then back to bed. Noel enjoyed her huge music collection on her smartphone. Roy went to work. She could hear him talking to customers in his office.

Cindy was fine with giving her three hundred dollars. Cindy would not settle for anything less than that. Not even for being a friend.

With the money, Noel could keep her unlimited music for a month or two.

Just like the radio, there were small breaks in the music app. Commercials about other things besides deals for a random store. What a nice break.

She looked around for the yarn balls since she settled on the designs for both commissions. Noel searched for the right herbs. What color would she choose for Cindy's bear even though the design was the same? Why choose the same colors as her first commission? She frowned.

Cindy would never know that her commission was a duplicate.

The clock said 5 am December 8th, Thursday. When did it turn 5 am?

Heavy footsteps dragged across the floor. "Go to bed, Noel."

# A Life For A Purse

"I guess I should," Noel left everything where it was and crawled into bed.  There was a mess but she would handle everything tomorrow.

The stuffing and stiches on her teddy bears were together.  Noel's finger stung from the needle she accidently poked herself with.  The outfits took the longest to put together.  Yellow and white shirts with light red pants.  To top everything off, she made small red hats for both of them.  Both bears smelled like lavender.

Noel took her cell phone off of her bed.  There were text messages coming from both Roy and Stephanie.  Both text messages told her to come downstairs.  Noel put on some clothes and walked down the stairs.  Stephanie and Roy were together.  This time, Roy had on a shirt and sweat pants.  This was a serious conversation.

Noel pulled up a chair and then she sat down, bracing the full on conversation that was coming.  "Look, Stephanie.  I'm sorry-"

"Sorry doesn't pay the bills.  I'm tired of helping a freeloader."

"Steph, we can pay the bills with no issues."  Stephanie shot her husband a glance but he continued, "Money isn't the issue here.  Not even for a year."  Roy placed his huge cup on to the table.

# A Life For A Purse

Stephanie folded her arms, "Forget this. I just got off of work. It's 7 pm and it's December the sixteenth. Are we discussing our Christmas list or not? Oh wait, one of us shouldn't be spending any money."

"Steph, we talked about this."

"I can handle my own money like I have been for months." Noel frowned, realizing how long it has been since she saw her cousin's face.

"I'm glad. You can work on your social skills, Noel. I've said hi to you several times and you never responded." Roy took a sip from his cup.

Noel shook her head, trying to recall what she did in the last few days beside work on her commissions and occasionally look up job openings. "I don't remember."

"What I want for Christmas is for you to stop being so cheap. It's not fair that I pay all the bills in this place and Robert cleans the house. Y-you? You're getting double the gifts as usual. I know it."

"Are we having this conversation, Steph? I thought we were discussing responsibilities and not childhood jealousy."

"So what? What about the bills, Stephanie?" Noel took a deep breath. Stephanie scooted her seat next to her husband. So much different than when she was alone with her. Was her cousin afraid of her?

# A Life For A Purse

"We've been waiting for you to move out for years. What you did a few days ago brought me back to when you gave me that black eye. I put on so much make up for work I was almost late."

Roy through his arm over Stephanie's shoulders. "You've been making a lot of noise. Almost enough to distract me from my work. The excuses that I had to make while on the phone…. I'm running out of them. We still need to make room for our future baby." Both Stephanie and Roy looked like a perfect couple.

"I know." This conversation was getting Noel nowhere. "I just want money or a gift card this year." Or a permanent job but that was not something she wanted to admit to them.

"I know. There's a nice place called Jessicas. There's a brand new purse coming out. I'll give you the flyer-"

"A purse? You have rolls of them." Noel remembered the rolls of purses in Stephanie's closet back at her mother's house and now.

"I just want you to feel better and not make so much noise at night. I know you can get so carried away upstairs. Don't worry about me, Noel."

"Roy. When are you going to stop being so…so modest? It's painful." Stephanie scooted away from her husband and checked her watch.

# A Life For A Purse

Noel thought about the long lines in stores right now. Anything that was popular was already gone and underneath a Christmas tree. "What if I can't get you that name brand purse?"

Stephanie folded her arms and smiled. "Well, if you can't afford it or the upcoming bills then you're out. There are nice apartments near here. Apartments that you could live in. I don't care which one you pick. We feel that you're not putting any effort into finding a new place."

"I-I have school loans to put up with. You know that. Why a purse?" Was there a way Noel could end this conversation? "What about the bills?"

"Because my appearance is everything. If I don't match the environment than I get fired. I've had this purse for three months. That is far too long, Noel. What kind of person do you both think I am? Just get me the purse and I won't kick you out in three months. Maybe in six months." Stephanie stood up from her spot. She held up a pocket mirror and held it close to her face while making her way up the stairs.

"That did not go as well as planned."

"What?" Noel stood up along with Roy.

"I always thought it would be cool to be a Christmas baby. I still do. Steph's been stressed. She's feeling down about her parents again."

"That fire was ages ago!" Noel's voice was louder than she anticipated it to be.

# A Life For A Purse

Roy's eyes widened.  "She doesn't know how to relax and she's not making any sense.  That's another thing.  I'll try to lighten her up.  Just buy the purse and you can start paying bills next month.  We'll decide which one."

"Right..."

Noel placed the stuffed animals on her bed.  Did Stephanie think that these stuffed animals were for her?  Did her cousin keep anything she made for her?  The scent was strong.  Had she put too much lavender inside of them?

Something stuck itself to Noel's feet as she took a step back.  Noel picked up the paper.  Jessica's was clearly at the top.  Was she really going to buy the purse for her cousin?  Stephanie never went back on her words.  Would she really throw her out if she did not buy a purse for her?

Noel placed the stuffed animals on her table.  This room was for Roy and Stephanie's future child?  She had spent too much time here.

Cindy needed to get rid of a roommate if Noel had any chances of moving out.  Placing the teddy bears on the table, Noel looked over her text messages.  "I've been so busy Noel.  The kids are way too excited for Christmas.  It's no way near that."

"How's my stuffed animal coming along?"

# A Life For A Purse

Noel took on of the bears and set it aside. She then positioned the stuffed bear and took a snap shot with her phone. Knowing Cindy, she was asleep.

"I think I can figure something out. My old roommate is leaving soon. She's going to college despite my pleas. College for art? That's a waste of her time but she wouldn't listen. Not everyone can be like you."

"Kids are oddly acting a lot better now. I don't get it. A coworker told them about coals in their gifts. I can't believe that worked. Oh well."

"What do you want for Christmas?"

Noel smiled. Something she had not done in a long time. "My own place."

She texted that of and fell asleep. Her laptop automatically shut off. Her web browser had been on a job application for a long time.

Noel stepped out of bed. The flyer stuck to her feet again. Realizing she did not get a good look at that flyer, she picked it up again. The purse was in a line with other similar purses. All one of a kind.

FOR SALE and for half off. One time event? A name brand she never recognized. Not even when she bothered staring at the rows of retired purses Stephanie had in her closet.

# A Life For A Purse

Maybe Noel could buy the purse online. She turned the computer on and searched. The laptop had fallen asleep on the screen where she held her job application form. She then opened another tab and typed in the website for Jessica's. The webpage opened to a variety of stores.

There were stores lined up. One of the locations, she recognized as the new shopping district next to her Wal-Mart. That location was a pain to drive to.

Noel continued searching. The scrolling images on the website caught her attention. There, the purses were stacked up, just like in the flyer. She could buy the purse online and avoid the shopping disasters. Paying for bills was better than waiting in line for that purse.

The page loaded. There was the price. Half off at 500 dollars! That was way more than the majority of her commission money. Did Noel just make stuffed animals in order to pay for her sister's vanity issues?

Noel scrolled down, looking for the ad to cart button. The button read only in select stores. Underneath was a description about each purse being unique and designed by some designer. The bags could be customized with extra parts. The date was the twentieth and at midnight.

Spending time outside of a store in the freezing cold with strangers for a purse? What was her life coming to?

Noel felt like her time at White Wolf had destroyed her chances of finding a job soon. How long would it be before she got another job? One last time with this IT job

# A Life For A Purse

application.  She filled in her name and the rest of the application. And then groaned when she saw the assessment test at the end.

When she was done answering the same elaborate questions over and over again, she pushed aside her laptop and closed her eyes.  The sent from the teddy bears entered her nose.  She should ship off this teddy bear soon.  Was Noel's time wasted?  Was there was way she could make her business into a full-time job or even part-time?

Then there were more bills and more bills.  Noel stood up, remembering her packaging materials were inside of the closet.  One quick message to the client on Creative Heaven's website and then she closed her laptop.

Noel walked across the post office's parking lot. She had spent some time waiting for a place to park her car. A car accident had caused a long wait for a parking spot in addition to the holiday season.

Inside the post office was the longest line she had ever seen for the place.  If Noel did not fill out the job application, then the line would have had been shorter. She held the medium sized box underneath her arm and walked to the end of the line.  The line reached outside of the next room and nearly reached the entrance.

# A Life For A Purse

At least Noel could read these while the line was stagnant. This beat staring at people miserably holding boxes.

"I should have guessed, Noel. You can't catch a break at your place. I'm working on it."

"I know. Cindy. I can't wait." Noel texted her response while keeping an eye on the moving line.

Christmas decorations filled up the next sliding door. The sliding door opened, allowing her into the room where the mail clerks were scanning packages. Random children began crying. A pregnant woman held one of her kids; she then stopped and began holding her stomach.

"Anyone willing to drop off their packages?" A mail clerk leaned over a counter near Noel. Noel looked at her package and the pregnant lady. She walked over, handed her the item, and then she finally walked out the post office.

The car accident turned into two angry women pointing at the dents in their cars on the far side of the building. A bystander pointed his phone at the argument.

That was probably a viral video in the making.

Noel walked toward her car, hoping that the item would make its destination unharmed by the hurrying post office workers. She opened her car and began driving.

Hobos walked around on top of the concrete islands. They held up empty boots walking past parked cars. One

# A Life For A Purse

had a child with him.  Noel rolled up her windows.  The cold air was giving her goosebumps.

"Good evening.  This is Rodney with United Technologies.  Is this Noel White?  Did I catch you at a bad time?"

"No.  I'm sorry.  Just worn out from Christmas joy."  The cold from outside stiffened her hands.  Noel fumbled with her phone, trying to steady her hands.

"I understand that feeling.  We are hosting job interviews after the holidays.  We'd thought you'd be a perfect fit."

No reference to White Castle?

"We have your resume.  Is this one recent?"  Was this interview from one of the job applications she filled out not too long ago?

"Yes.  That's a recent resume."  Noel finally steadied her hands.  Blood was rushing to her digits and she firmly held her phone with both hands.

"How about we set you up for January the third?  All ready and refreshed for the new year?"

Noel brought up her enthusiastic voice.  "That's perfect."  She poked Cindy's stuffed animal in the nose, hoping that none of the stitching would come out at all.

# A Life For A Purse

"We'll see you there. Take care." The phone call ended.

Noel looked at the date on the flyer. The water ran through her fingers for over a minute. She remembered looking at her hand during phone calls. Could she go through another tech job and for how long? Would she be able to stay focused on the phone calls?

Cindy would like this bear. Noel wanted to personally hand the bear to her best friend. She wrote in big letters on a piece of paper right next to the bear: For Cindy. Right now, she had to go buy that purse for her cousin.

How long was this going to take? The flyer said this was a midnight sale. Roy passed by her room in a white shirt with tiny holes throughout the shirt.

"Hey Noel? We're starting with the water bill later on. Those showers of yours are really long."

"Ok." There was nothing she could say about that. She always ran the water for a long time. "Well, I have an upcoming interview."

Roy stopped walking. Stephanie was snoring not so far off.

"What company?" He was walking toward his home office.

"United…Technologies?" It took a moment to recall that name.

# A Life For A Purse

Roy raised his eyebrows but ignored her question. "I've never worked there. I'm sure Steph will be happy to hear this. Well, I have to work now."

Noel gave a forced and lazy smile and turned around. There was a phone call coming from Cindy.

"Hey Noel, It's the last day before this break. It's been really hard but these kids need me."

"I hope I never understand that." Noel lied down on her bed again.

"You still don't like children? You haven't changed since High School."

"I like saving money. Healthcare plans are so expensive. Can you imagine supporting children underneath those? Cindy?"

"I know. It sounds like a nightmare but you don't understand."

Noel decided to change the subject. "I have another job interview."

"Oh. You do?" There was no excitement in her voice unlike everyone else. "Doing what? I thought you wanted to pursue your dreams this time."

Noel looked to Cindy's stuffed bear. "Doing IT again."

# A Life For A Purse

"Really?  Why would you that again and again?  It's not your thing and you know that.  I could cover you once my roommate leaves."

"I'm paying bills now.  Like the water bill."  Noel skipped out on talking about the purse.  The idea was so ridiculous that she did not want to bother bringing Stephanie's vanity issues up.

"Oh... I see.  Well that sucks.  Is this job permanent?  Not one of those temp jobs again?"

Noel smiled.  "This one is permanent one this time. I think I have a plan.  Maybe I could build my business again like I used to.  Just because I have a job.  Doesn't mean I can't work Creative Heaven."

"I'm glad you feel that way.  I'm sort of always here to help.  The kids are going to be too excited before this big break."  Cindy sounded disappointed.

Cindy was not asking about her teddy bear.  Maybe Noel could lighten up the mood.  "You'll be free on Christmas, right?"

"O-Of course!  Why?"

"I wanna give you your bear.  I think you'll love it."

Cindy screamed.  "That's perfect.  I can't wait to see it.  I wish didn't have to work in the morning but I have to go."

Noel smiled.  "Goodnight Cindy."

# A Life For A Purse

Noel put her phone down and stepped on the floor to inspect her stuffed animal. The thing was not scented at all

The reason customers brought her stuff was for the scents. she would have to take the shirt off. That was a lot of work. Maybe she could sell this one for a smaller price. She saw the stiching. There was still work to be done. Someone at Creative Heaven would love the stuffed bear if she continued making it.

Noel closed her door. There was noises coming from the Roy's office and Stephanie was still snoring. What a perfect time to just slip out of the house. Noel had made her way toward her car. Roy was busy working and sounded like he was in an argument with a customer. Why not show that she had the ability to work?

Noel walked toward her car and prepared to drive away. There were people already on the road at this hour. Why did that surprise her at all? Noel sighed and kept driving. No homeless people this time.

Noel turned into the Wal-Mart and then down the path which lead to the shopping center. Jessica's was in the middle of two white buildings like on the flyer. She drove around the parking lot, looking for a free space. There was a spot at the far end of the parking lot. She took that spot.

A little walking would not hurt her. Already, there was a long line forming by the door. No one had anything else to do besides go shopping these days?

# A Life For A Purse

"Oh my goodness. I can't wait. Open the door already." A hefty woman squealed and squealed again. Her friend placed a hand on her shoulder, hoping that her friend would stop squealing. That did nothing.

There were similar conversations going on around the store's entrance. Noel felt a little awkward going alone as she walked behind these women as well. Her watch read ten o clock. Was this a popular event or not? Cindy would not be able to join her.

"This line is for the whole event?" Noel asked the squealing woman. She took the opportunity to look like she was a part of the conversation at the front of the line.

"Yep. Marco Rossi designed a lot of these beautiful purses. Good thing this is small, boring Virginia. No one cares about us. My friend in New York can barely make it into a Jessica's store no matter what time of day it is." The woman breath slowly, obviously out of breathes from her excitement.

So far no one was making a fuss about Noel skipping the line. "I'm here for my cousin."

"Oh...you're getting your cousin a gift? That's really sweat of you." The woman was calmer now since she was trying to regain her posture.

"Right. The prices were too high online and she wouldn't stop talking about this purse, so I'm here." Would the woman believe her lie? She forgot to see if the purses were available anywhere else.

# A Life For A Purse

"Too high? Those scalpers on eBay ruin everything." The woman's friend was scrolling through her phone. She turned her phone around, pointing at the rows of purses on sale for more than six grand.

"Yeah, that's what I'm talking about." Noel looked around. Nobody cared that she skipped the line after all. She smiled.

The woman shook her head and went back to browsing on the app. "It's a good thing you came here."

That was something that she could agree on. She laughed along with the women. Noel watched a truck in the distance park in one of the few parking spaces for the store. There were several men in the car. None got out of the truck. It was freezing after all.

In the store, the sight of someone walking toward the store caught her eye. A store attendant walked to the side of the door and pressed a few buttons. The glass doors slide open. Noel quickly made her way to the side of the door, not wanting to be in the way of the crowd. She looked around, searching for the purses.

The purses were right there in the middle of the aisle. There were several people right beside her. Stephanie had never mentioned the color that she wanted so she just grabbed a purse. By the time she looked back, half of the purses were gone. She held on to this purse and walked toward the cash register.

The sliding doors were open again. Noel made her purchase. The man walked in. Was he one of the guys who

# A Life For A Purse

were sitting inside of the trucks? The man was wearing a black jacket and a mask over his head. Black everything; as if this man was planning on robbing the store. Is this a joke?

Noel walked along the side of the store by the clothing section. She did not want anything to do with that man. Would the clothes hide her from this man's view? Some women stopped their activities and looked at the man. He had one hand in his pocket. Noel forced herself to keep walking silently toward the exit.

There was a loud pop in the air. Some women screamed. The man did have a gun! Noel was relieved to start seeing the glass window. Two loud pops and something hit the ground with a loud stud.

"Anybody else want to play hero?"

Noel held on to her purse, passed the last line clothes, and ran out the sliding doors. She wanted the gunshots to stop. Noel's foot came in contact with a speed bumper. Her face hit the ground hard. From the distance, Noel could hear a few people getting out of a vehicle.

Noel stopped herself from screaming and lifted herself off of the bumper. If she could run faster, she could make it to her car. With the purse underneath her arms, she bolted in the direction of her car.

Another loud gunshot. Noel took another step on her right leg and fell on to the street again. Noel looked into the sky, blood flowing from the hole in her right leg.

# A Life For A Purse

Her back covered the purse completely. Footsteps approached her.

"Get off the purse, Bitch!"

Noel opened her mouth to speak but gibberish came out. The pain was too much. Everything did not feel real.

The man kneeled down, touched her waist. Noel gasped and swung her hand. Her hand came in contact with what seemed like his face. "No!"

Noel felt a blow to her face. Hands touched her waist again. Noel swung her hands wildly. She grabbed something and pulled. The cotton came off and her vision finally returned to her.

Four men dressed in black stood around her.

"What the hell Sean? Get the damn purse."

"She took my mask, man. She took my mask!"

"No shit. Kill her. We need that dam purse, Sean. And she's fucking on it."

Were these voices coming from the other men in the parking lot? They stood around her while she breathed in and out. The unmasked man placed his foot on her stomach, pinning her down with pressure. Noel's eyes and moth widened. The pain from her gunshot wound increased.

# A Life For A Purse

"You got it." Sean pointed the kneeled down, pointing the barrel directly into Noel's forehead. Before Noel could react, she felt nothing.

## EPILOUGE

Stephanie placed her hand on her cousin's doorway. Roy walked passed her and to his office. It was not nighttime but she knew her husband needed a break from today. Not everyone goes to a funeral on Christmas day. Instead of opening presents, she was staring at Noel's empty bed. The room was the same as the night Noel left for Jessica's.

That teddy bear was still there. A piece of paper with Cindy written on it lay underneath the bear. That woman came to the funeral dressed in a black shirt and black jeans. Hair dyed blue as well. If Stephanie did not guess that the woman was Noel's best friend, she would have had someone escort her off the property.

Cindy did ask for this teddy bear. Stephanie wanted to feel the same level of excitement for her cousin's hobby.

While connected to a charger, Noel's phone vibrated. Soon, Noel's phone bill would be overdue and Stephanie would not be able to hear this phone vibrate again and again.

# A Life For A Purse

Stephanie stepped into the room. The police let her keep the phone. Was her cousin really dead? Her cousin's casket was closed during the funeral. Her injuries distorted her face and her aunt was the only one who saw Noel's face.

On Christmas Eve, Stephanie waited outside of the door, in the funeral home, as her aunt looked at Noel's face. When her aunt left the room, the woman's skin was pale. No one should have to see Noel's face.

Her own phone vibrated as she walked toward Noel's phone. "Stephanie. You're going to work soon." Her aunt did not ask a question. This was a demand.

Stephanie looked at the white ceiling through her oncoming tears. "No. I still have sick days."

"For fuck's sake. It's not your fault, Stephanie!" As usual, her aunt's voice was loud.

"I literally told her I'd throw her out for a purse. She really believed me. How was I supposed to know? How was I supposed to know?"

Stephanie held her own phone to her ear despite her aunt's volume. Noel's phone kept vibrating. Her cousin's screen was lighting up with notifications from Creative Heaven. The messages read Commission Requests. Was Noel making real money from her hobby?

"You're a full grown women. Noel wasn't the best daughter but you don't joke like that. There's too many

# A Life For A Purse

homeless people wondering the streets as of late. Have you seen them?"

Stephanie put her back to the wall and slide down to the ground. Her stomach tightened. She held Noel's phone and pressed on the power button. The phone powered off, ending the constant notifications.

"Why was I set on that purse?" Stephanie placed her hands on her forehead. If she had on makeup, she would have been concerned about ruining her face. She had not put on makeup since a police officer delivered the news to her front door.

"You can't….change time. You can't put out fires or stop crazy people with guns. We've been over this again and again. I will not repeat myself. You go to work tomorrow before you lose your house. Do you-"

Stephanie choked her phone across the room. The new case Roy brought her protected her phone from breaking against the wall. The phone bounced off of the wall and landed on the floor perfectly fine. Her aunt was not helping her. Did her aunt grieve her own daughter's death at all?

The phone vibrated again. Stephanie stared at it and then at the teddy bear on the table. Only a few days ago, she believed her cousin was making her a teddy bear. The pillows, teddy bears, and blankets Noel made for her was thrown away before Stephanie agreed to take Noel with her. What good was it for a gull grown woman to have to those items in her home?

# A Life For A Purse

How could Stephanie let anyone see these children toys?

Now, Stephanie only had this messy room to remember Noel.

"Steph!"

Roy stood by the doorway. "Noel's friend's at the door."

"Let her stay there. I'm busy."

"Steph? Cindy needs the bear and that's it."

Stephanie lifted herself from her spot. "I doubt she needs it. No one needs her stuff." Stephanie walked toward the bear and grabbed it by the hand.

"We talked about this Steph. We talked about this." Roy stepped aside, letting Stephanie pass him.

"I know." Stephanie continued down the hallway and down the stairs.

What did everyone else see in Noel that she did not?

Stephanie reached the bottom of the stairs. The doorbell rang. She opened the door.

"Hi…You're Stephanie?" Cindy stood before her in sweat pants and a sweat shirt. Stephanie wanted to say something about her state of dress but she decided not to. Her face felt terrible from the lack of makeup.

"Yes…"

# A Life For A Purse

"Oh…ok. Well, I'm here for the teddy bear." The woman looked around. "Is that it?" Her voice was a strange mix of excitement and sadness.

Stephanie lifted up the teddy bear. The scent entered her nose. The scent was not as nauseating as she remembered it to be.

"It smells great." Immediately, the teddy bear was grabbed. Cindy took it into her arms and cuddled it. Sniffed it. Stephanie made a face.

Cindy looked at Stephanie and laughed. "I know she always told me to stop doing that but I can't help it. I love these that much. I'll treasure it forever."

Stephanie watched the woman enjoy the teddy bear. For a moment, she thought of how excited she used to get when talking to her cousin. That was back when she was living with her aunt.

Cindy held the teddy bear as if it was her baby. "This wasn't how I wanted to spend my time today. But this is Noel I'm talking about. Well, I'll get going now. I know you're glad to see me and this thing go. Bye."

Had Noel told this woman how much she hated her? Stephanie could not think of a response. She was too shocked to answer back. Instead, she stared as Cindy stepped down the stairs, still cuddling the teddy bear.

It was only a bear. Why was tears forming in her eyes again?

# A Life For A Purse

"Hey!"

Cindy stopped by her car which was parked behind Roy's truck. "Yes...?"

"What was Noel like?"

Cindy eyes widened. She opened the passenger's seat on her car and put her teddy bear inside. The seat belt fit the teddy bear perfectly.

"What was she like?" Cindy walked over to the other side of her car and opened her door. "What was she like?"

Why was this woman repeating herself? "Yes. My cousin. You heard me right?"

"Yeah, you're cousin? I'm not...I'm not answering that. You should know. Goodbye." Cindy sat inside of the car, closed the door, and then started her car. She pulled out of the driveway, frowning.

Stephanie watched Noel's best friend disappear from her sight. Cold air hit her body. A car drove off in the distance. Her stomach knotted again and her vision became blurry from tears. What happened to her and her cousin's relationship?

# A Life For A Purse

## What Did You Think of A Life of For A Purse?

Tiffany writes alone and only has her editors' advice on what she can do to improve her writing. Having readers express their opinions through reviews would mean a lot to her; rather the review is constructive, negative, or really positive. There is no pressure to write a review and follow her work on Amazon.

Everyone's time is valuable.

# A Life For A Purse

## <u>About the Author</u>

Tiffany enjoyed spending a majority of her childhood living in her head. She made the choice to share her wild imaginations with the world in 2017. Although Tiffany enjoys writing romantic fantasy, she sometimes writes stories based in reality.

Made in the USA
Middletown, DE
07 July 2019